Easter Time

Retold by Laura Kelly
Illustrated by Eugenie Fernandes

Palm Sunday

"In the village ahead you will find a colt," Jesus said to his friends. "Untie it and bring it here."

Can you help Jesus' friends find their way to the colt?

Jesus' friends found the colt, just as Jesus said.

Can you find the colt and three other animals hidden in the picture?

As Jesus rode the colt into Jerusalem, people cheered and spread their cloaks and palm branches in front of him.

They shouted, "Blessed be the one who comes in the name of the Lord!"

Can you find five things wrong with this picture?

The Last Supper

Jesus and his friends had a special Passover meal.

B-2   A-3   A-2

C-1   C-2   A-1

B-3   B-1   C-3

A	B	C

Copy the pattern in each square onto the correct square of the grid. You'll discover a picture!

Jesus told his friends that we should serve one another. Then he knelt down and washed his friends' feet.

This picture is a mirror image of the opposite page but there are five differences. Can you find them all?

Gethsemane

After the meal, Jesus and his friends went to the Garden of Gethsemane.

Jesus prayed while his friends slept.

Color the picture.

Jesus is arrested

One of Jesus' followers, Judas, betrayed Jesus for a bag of silver coins.

These pictures of Judas are very similar, but only two are identical. Can you find the two that are exactly the same?

Judas told the temple guards where they could find Jesus. Follow the maze to see where they found him.

Jesus' trial

The guards brought Jesus before the Pharisees, the leaders of the Jewish people.

Can you find these two
Pharisees in the picture?

A ruler named Pilate asked Jesus "Are you the
_ _ _ _ of the Jews?"

To find a clue to the missing word, use a yellow
crayon to color in every space that contains a dot.

The Crucifixion

Jesus was sentenced to die on a cross.

Color the picture.

The Resurrection

On the Sunday after Jesus died, some women went to the tomb with spices for his body.

Color the picture.

Someone appeared to the women and said to them, "Jesus is not here. He has risen just as he said!"

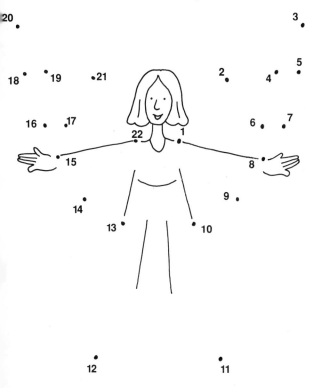

Connect the dots to find out who appeared to the women.

The women told Jesus' friends about the angel.
Peter and John ran to see for themselves.

Help Peter and John find their way to the tomb.

That same day, Jesus appeared to two of his
followers on a journey. But the followers did not
know it was Jesus until later, when he sat down
to eat with them.

Can you find five things wrong with this picture?

Jesus then appeared to his friends.

They were overjoyed to see Jesus alive again,
just as he had promised.

Can you find the five differences between these
two pictures?

The Ascension

Jesus stayed on earth for forty days. Then he took his friends to the top of a hill, and as they were talking, Jesus went up into Heaven on the clouds. Two angels came and said to his friends, "Jesus will come back someday, the same way you have seen him leave!"

Color the picture.